"If cats wore bumper stickers, Skeeter's would read 'Question Authority.' He's everywhere, expressing his opinions, giving and demanding affection, and bending the rules. More than once, I've decided there must be two of him."

When a stray kitten romps into Lynne's life, she has no idea what she's getting into. As Lynne describes in letters to her friend Angie, Skeeter is all cat—high-spirited, contrary, and inventive. He's so goofy that he reminds Lynne of her own nuttiest escapades; so irrepressible that even Lynne's neighbor, Mark, gets wound around his paw. And when Angie visits to see Skeeter for herself. . . . Well, no one who meets Skeeter will ever be quite the same again.

Author Online!

For more about Anne L. Watson
and her books, please visit her at

www.annelwatson.com

Also by Anne L. Watson

Joy

Pacific Avenue

Flight (forthcoming)

Anne L. Watson

Skeeter

A Cat Tale

Shepard & Piper
Olympia, Washington
2005

Copyright © 2005 Anne L. Watson
All rights reserved.

ISBN-13: 978-0-938497-51-6
ISBN-10: 0-938497-51-0

Library of Congress Control Number: 2004117048
Library of Congress subject headings:
Cats—Fiction

2.1

For my beloved critters

1
Dear Angie

October 6, 1999

Dear Angie,

I made it back to California without mishap or even a traffic ticket, although I was eligible for speeding tickets in every state along the route. That was the quickest move of my whole life. Thanks for helping me pack. Also for pointing out that I'd better not dither and procrastinate much longer if I expected to make it over the Rockies in decent weather. I must have lived in L.A. too long—it wouldn't have occurred to me to plan for snow.
    The offer to take back my California job was irresistible. But I enjoyed Chicago, even in the winter. I'm going to miss it. I'll miss you, too. Don't quit keeping the place stirred up just because I'm gone. I'm counting on you.
    The trip was amazing. Did I tell you that, when I moved from California in 1997, I had my car shipped? This time I couldn't afford to do that, and I wasn't looking forward to driving. I don't know what I expected—city traffic all the way, maybe. But it turned out to be fun. I started wondering whether I even want my old job. Maybe I'll get a truck-driving license and go back and forth.

I got to Lincoln the first night. That seemed far enough. The next morning I started early, only to get caught in fog on the freeway. It was too thick for me to see any exits, so I couldn't get off. All I could do was hope there wasn't anything slow in front of me or anything fast behind me. Eventually it cleared. I made it to Cheyenne by afternoon, though I got a little lost.

I could see I wasn't making good enough time, so I got a dawn start the next morning and reached Elko by night. Over six hundred miles—ouch! The next night, I was in Monterey, exhausted. It was out of my way but I wanted to see some friends there before I settled down in L.A. Somehow, once I'm working, I can never get away.

I spent a couple of days with them, then drove down to Long Beach. I'm staying with my friend Nancy here till I find a place. I think I'll look in San Pedro. It's always been my favorite town in the L.A. area. Right on the beach, but not too expensive.

Back to work tomorrow! Thanks again for your help.

Love,
Lynne

October 15, 1999

Dear Angie,

    I've gotten settled at Nancy's now. My furniture and boxes aren't coming for a couple of weeks, so I'll have time to find an apartment first. For now, I only have what I could carry in the car. I brought necessities—clothes, books, my CD player, and the coffeepot. I forgot a few items like towels and sheets, but those are easy to borrow.
    I've known Nancy for years, so it's like coming home to stay with her. Her household is awash with cats, dogs, and relatives, but somehow everyone manages.
    Work is interesting, but of course more high-stress than I've been used to. Too many jobs to do at once. Besides, Nancy's house is in Long Beach, an hour—or more—commute each way. I'm so harried, I would scream—if I could find the time.
    I'm going apartment hunting this weekend. If I can find something in San Pedro, it would cut my commute in half. Also, there are plenty of old buildings there, which I like better than new ones.
    I'll write again when I find an apartment.

Love,
Lynne

October 21, 1999

Dear Angie,

I found a place! It's in the part of San Pedro called Point Fermin—lots of fine old buildings and a beach. Well, a sort of beach. A cliff plunges down to a cobble strand—stark but spectacular. When the waves break, they toss those stones around with a noise like dumping a load of bricks. On the cliff top, there's a park with a bandstand, and even a Victorian lighthouse.

My apartment is in a two-story building from about the same era. There are only four apartments, two upstairs and two down. My place has big rooms, oak floors, redwood cabinets, and a dining room. Also nine-foot ceilings.

And the landlady says I can have a cat! It's against the lease, but I asked anyway. She said, "Well . . . we-don't-really-allow-pets-in-the-apartments" (more or less one word), "but . . ."—looking at a black cat sunning on the porch—"I see Armando has one. There's a stray kitten hanging around my nephew's house. I'll take you over there tomorrow, if you want to see about it."

She made it clear I don't have to take this particular kitten, but I think I'll go look at it. The price will be right, and maybe it'll be a good one.

I'll be moving November 1. Till then, I'll be at Nancy's.

Love,
Lynne

November 3, 1999

Dear Angie,

    Moving day was crazy, but then, what else is new? Nancy helped, and we hired a couple of guys. I'm sort of settled. The living room is still full of boxes, but the kitchen stuff and clothes are unpacked.
    I adopted that kitten! I wasn't looking for such a young one, and I think it's a male, but it's a sweetie. It's a gray tabby with white markings on the legs, head, and tummy. It was already housebroken, so no problems there. I named it Skeeter, which is a Southernism for "mosquito," in case you don't know. The way it circles and whines is just like one.
    The neighbors are friendly—also quiet, thank goodness. There's a family downstairs, and single guys live in the other two apartments. I think the downstairs guy has a steady girlfriend. I share a utility room with the guy in the other upstairs apartment. I have a washer and dryer, but the only hookups are on his side. So we're going to cooperate. He's a children's author, and he works at home. He doesn't seem too crazy about cats. But he's OK, I think.
    Work is about the same. There's always more than enough of it to go around.

How are you? How's the office? Did they hire anyone to replace me, or are you doing both our jobs?

                    Love,
                    Lynne

November 9, 1999

Dear Angie,

    Mark, the guy in the other upstairs apartment, invited me to go downtown with him to see the Pompeii exhibit at the L.A. County Museum. We wanted to get there early, because of the crowds. Good thing we left in plenty of time, because we got held up by a parade before we were even out of San Pedro.
    First a policeman motorcycled up and stopped traffic. Then an almost-in-tune brass band marched past us. A disorganized swarm of people followed, mostly in ordinary clothes, some dressed in red, white, and green for a fiesta.
    Arches of helium balloons echoed the festival colors, swaying in the offshore breeze. Six men carried the Virgin of Guadeloupe on a small platform, followed by more people, more balloons. The parade was past.
    Mark said they were probably on their way to bless the fishing fleet. I sent a blessing of my own to the boats—not that I think I could make a difference to their safety or their catch, but it made me feel good to do it.
    Parades are common here, especially near the holidays. They used to have a boat parade at Christmas, but I haven't heard anything about it this year.

Maybe it's too early. I missed it there in Chicago last year. When I asked if there would be a boat parade, my family looked at me like I was crazy. "Lynne," my sister said, "this time of year, the lake's *frozen*." Scratch the boat parade.

    Nancy came over to meet Skeeter. She says he's a boy. He isn't going to remain one for long, though. I can't have a tomcat in the house.

Love,
Lynne

November 15, 1999

Dear Angie,

I keep buying toys for Skeeter, hoping to find something he'll enjoy. Most cat toys bore him. He plays with a chosen few, and also has stolen a couple of my possessions: a furry computer mouse cover someone gave me, and my floppy stuffed dog Wolfie, just the size for Skeeter to fight with.

Once in a while, a toy scares him. That was the trouble with the feathered mouse. If his problem had been aesthetic, I would have understood it, since the thing was hideous. However, I couldn't see why he was afraid of it.

I dangled it in front of him. He gave it a horrified look and ran. I tied it to a string and pulled it across his path. He hid. I decided he needed time to get used to it and left it in the hallway. It stayed there for several days, seemingly untouched. He wasn't getting used to it.

When I got home from work yesterday, the feathered mouse had disappeared. It wasn't under anything, or behind anything. It wasn't anywhere.

I know what happened, of course. Skeeter watched me drive away in the morning and when he was sure I was gone, went into the hallway and stood by the feathered mouse. In an annoyed way—this was almost more trouble than it was worth—he stood on his hind legs and began to grow like the Christmas tree in *The Nutcracker*. By degrees, he turned into a ten-year-old boy, the kind of boy who would be nicknamed "Skeeter." I can see him now, hazel eyes, sandy hair, and freckles. His transformation complete, he bent and grabbed the feathered mouse, unlocked the back door, took it downstairs, and threw it into the garbage can.

Then he returned in a hurry. I rarely come back home once I've left, but once in a while I do. He closed and locked the back door. With a sigh of relief, he turned back into a cat.

How else could it have happened?

Love,
Lynne

November 20, 1999

Dear Angie,

Skeeter never does anything without a reason. There may not be much point, but there always is a *reason*, if only I can find it.

I'm still puzzling over his nighttime antics, though. I wish I could ask him what he thinks he's doing.

I go to bed early. Skeeter does not. This is normal, since cats are more or less nocturnal. My bedtime coincides with his high-energy evening play session, so I shut him out of the bedroom.

However, I usually wake in the middle of the night. As I wander down the hall to the bathroom, Skeeter sneaks into my bed.

When I return, he snuggles and purrs, the ideal cat. This is to fool me into letting him stay. Once he manages that, a demon gets hold of him. He jumps into the open window and yowls, then thunders back across my prone body to my desk, where he chews pencils and shreds all the paper he can get his paws on. Then he attacks the wind chime and the sewing basket. He sharpens his claws on the bed skirt, turns over the wastebasket, and raids my jewelry box.

At this point, I eject him from the bedroom and shut the door. He doesn't like this. It's a good thing he can't talk.

If he could, I'd undoubtedly have the same problem my friend Juanita got into with her bird. Juanita had parrots, lovebirds, cockatiels, and even a white cockatoo. But the bird that caused all the trouble was an ordinary-looking parakeet.

She was teaching this parakeet tricks, and he was doing well. He could balance on one foot, walk backwards, and do the loop-de-loo on his swing. She was also trying to teach him to talk, but without success. The bird wouldn't say anything but *awwwk, awwwk, awwwk*.

One morning she had a coffee party for some ladies from her church. The bird tried one of his tricks, and he took a header. He fell on his little blue tush and said, loudly and distinctly, "Oh, shit." He hadn't learned that word from *her*, but there was no way to tell that to the church ladies.

That would be the problem if Skeeter could talk— the things he'd say. I wouldn't want to be responsible for his language or his opinions. On the other hand, I'd be able to ask what he means by all those stupid antics in the middle of the night.

Love,
Lynne

November 30, 1999

Dear Angie,

I had Thanksgiving dinner with Mark's family. Since they live nearby, it wasn't a big deal. I was worried because it seemed like the wrong occasion to ask for vegetarian. But it turns out he's a veggie too, and so is his mom. That's California for you.

The holiday is over now. I'm back to nonstop work, chores, and errands. My first task this week was taking Skeeter to the animal birth control place to be fixed.

He had kept me awake for most of the night, and I was having a bleary time of it. A good many people had brought their pets, so the receptionist was busy. She gave me a tag to put on Skeeter's carrier. It had blanks for my name and address, daytime phone number, and a small line for "type." I asked what was supposed to go on the line.

"What kind of cat is it?" explained the receptionist.

What kind of cat is Skeeter? A short line like that wouldn't begin to cover it. And I was sure she had no time for that much information.

"He's just a cat," I said, and wrote C-A-T. They taught me to spell this in first grade. She looked in astonishment at what I'd written.

"Cat," I said helpfully, in case her first grade curriculum hadn't been the same as mine. With the L.A. Unified School District, you can never tell.

She looked at me like I was crazy and she had no time for a therapy session. She peered into the carrier, scratched out what I'd written, and wrote D-S-H above it.

The carrier looked official, sitting there with the tag on it. DSH? I know ORD, that's Chicago; and MSY, New Orleans. LAX is us, which has always seemed apt. But DSH?

"Wait," I said, "I don't want you to ship him anywhere. I want you to neuter him."

The receptionist was obviously having a bad morning too. Right behind me was an impatient guy who had brought a Rottweiler to be spayed.

"DSH stands for 'domestic shorthair,'" she told me, somewhat testily.

Well, this was wonderful news. I had thought Skeeter was just an alley cat. But now that I know he's a genuine domestic shorthair, I wonder if I made a mistake getting him neutered.

Love,
Lynne

December 2, 1999

Dear Angie,

    The earthquake didn't do any damage here. I know they say animals can predict them, but Skeeter didn't. Or at least if he did, he didn't tell me.
    But I predicted it. About ten days before it happened, I said I believed we'd have about a magnitude seven quake within two weeks. I said it in public, too, in front of witnesses. Everyone is impressed with me at the moment. I wish I thought I could do it again. An ability to predict earthquakes accurately would take care of my retirement. I'd live in a cottage over at Cal Tech and let them know when one was coming.
    The quake happened in the small hours of the morning. Skeeter usually sleeps in his own bed, but he happened to be in mine at the time—my bad luck. I was wakened less by the temblor than by the gyrations of a hissing, terrified cat. I came fully awake as he disappeared under the bed.
    This was a relief. Twenty-five years of owning cats in Southern California has taught me to avoid them in earthquakes. Their claws and teeth are far more hazardous than anything described in the pamphlets of the Governor's Office of Emergency Services. From a cat's point of view, humans are responsible for

everything. If the house is shaking, better bite your owner fast, to make it stop.

I looked out the window, keeping back from the glass a bit, just in case. The sky was alive with lightning-like flashes. There was no thunder, and a storm didn't seem too likely. The Northern Lights, on a holiday? Probably not. The temperature was about eighty. Electrical installations shorting out? Yes, that would do it. The wind chime tinkled, swinging eerily in the still air.

The earthquake lasted only a few seconds, but Skeeter kept the memory alive by pouting for several hours. He couldn't be convinced it wasn't some trick I had played on him. He finally emerged from under the bed, but he made it clear I was on probation, and I'd better not do it again.

And then last week, I got a private flash that Los Angeles might have a major quake in the year 2000. I hope it doesn't happen. Skeeter would never forgive me. And I'm not at all certain about those accommodations at Cal Tech.

Love,
Lynne

December 10, 1999

Dear Angie,

    Mark and I went to my friend Lisa's house. She has cats but they are not Skeeter-cats. They are pedigree Persians, lovely and expensive. Her halls are decked with red and blue award ribbons, and I wondered whether to point out that those colors were better for July 4 than for Christmas. I thought of suggesting she replace the blue with some green, but decided she wouldn't think it was funny.
    While Lisa and I gossiped, Mark petted a few of the champions. After we left, he confided that Lisa was OK, but he didn't like her cats as much as he likes Skeeter. I was surprised, since Skeet has been such a little hellion lately. What, I asked him, had Lisa's cats *done*? My imagination was running wild. Maybe they stole his hubcaps or picked his pocket. They'd have to be pretty extreme to outdo Skeeter.
    "They're just *fluffy*," he answered.
    I was confused. What did fur have to do with it?
    "They sit there like bath mats. They're just fluffy."

I explained that long-haired cats have been bred for laid-back dispositions so they will tolerate the grooming their fur requires. If Skeeter had long hair, we'd be in trouble. We'd have to hypnotize him and put it in cornrows.

Mark prefers a cat with personality. This is Skeeter, all right. If cats wore bumper stickers, Skeeter's would read "Question Authority." He's everywhere, expressing his opinions, giving and demanding affection, and bending the rules. More than once, I've decided there must be two of him.

Mark thinks I spoil Skeeter. He offers as evidence the cat-toy jungle in my apartment. Skeeter disagrees. *He* thinks he's treated like a Marine recruit, citing my refusal to let him climb the Christmas tree. I'm encouraged by their complaints, to tell the truth. I've always believed the surest sign I'm on the right track is that everybody is dissatisfied with me for different reasons.

Like Mark, though, I like Skeeter the way he is. At least I can tell him from the bath mat. Even if he dyes his fur as blue as my bath mat, to trick me, I'll know him every time. I'll know because the mat does not hook my ankle with its claws as I walk by, or yowl at my bedroom door at five-thirty every morning. Nor does it curl up on my chest in a warm snuggle or give me kitty kisses with a rough tongue. I'm onto him. He can't fool me.

                                      Love,
                                      Lynne

December 15, 1999

Dear Angie,

    I spent most of this morning cleaning the living room. Skeeter, who demands to be lifted when he wants to get on the bed, had somehow removed ornaments from high on the Christmas tree. He had played with them, then abandoned them under the couch. At least, I assume it was Skeeter. They surely didn't walk there on their own, and I can't imagine Mark doing something like that.
    Anyway, it reminded me of a visit to a client's home the other day. As a historic preservation consultant, I get to look at wonderful buildings and then write reports about them. It's a great job, but it occasionally takes me to some odd places, and this was one of them.
    When I entered the house, a Victorian in downtown Los Angeles, I immediately saw how messy and, well, dirty it was. I pretended not to notice. What else could I do?
    The client met with me in the living room, next to the Christmas tree. She had cats, many cats.
    One of them climbed about two thirds of the way up the tree and scooped a green glass bubble into his

paw. Then he lobbed the ornament exactly like a hand grenade, so it exploded right at my feet.

"Oh," said my client, "I didn't think he could climb so high."

The cat threw a gold one, missing me by inches.

"Naughty cat," she said, without conviction.

It wasn't easy to concentrate on the building with this feline terrorist after me. I finished my work quickly, one eye out for ambush.

Even then, I wasn't home free—she insisted on giving me lunch. The squalor made this a squeamish business. I managed to eat one bowl of soup, refused seconds, and escaped as soon as I could.

I had a different but even more curious lunch a couple of weeks ago with an author-illustrator friend of Mark's. My hostess was fascinating, the place was spotless, and the food was superb.

But halfway through the meal, she removed a vole from her freezer and passed it around so we could see it—we'd been talking about voles for some reason. She told us she uses frozen animals as models for her illustrations. No doubt this is a good idea, and she doesn't kill the animals, only puts them to good use if she happens to find one. But I couldn't help wondering what else she had in there, and whether the frozen zoo was kept separate from the food. I put it out of my mind and finished my soup. And asked for seconds.

The authors I've met so far are nice, but I think they can be a bit eccentric. Not crazy like my client, just different. And that's fine with me.

                                    Love,
                                    Lynne

December 20, 1999

Dear Angie,

    Thanks for the package! I'm saving it to open on Christmas Eve. I hope yours arrives on time. This year, I was a little late getting organized. Somehow I didn't believe it was really Christmas—it's been much too hot.
    Once I got into the holiday spirit, I wanted to go somewhere nicer than the mall. So I headed up to Beverly Hills. The old downtown is called "the Triangle," and it's always beautifully decorated for the holidays.
    This year was no exception—in fact, they'd gone all-out. The store windows glittered with fake snow, and all the street trees were decked with twinkling lights. There was even a group of carolers in Victorian dress, meandering along the sidewalk, pausing here and there to serenade the shoppers.
    I listened for a few minutes, learning, among other things, that the singers had seen their mothers kissing Santa Claus and that they were dreaming of a white Christmas. The latter sentiment was especially believable—the group was sweating it out in velvet costumes better suited to the North Pole than to southern California.

I did wonder briefly about the completely-secular song repertoire, but learned from a leaflet that the carolers' services were provided by the city government. So that little mystery was cleared up.

When I finished shopping, I stopped at a coffeehouse for a snack. The singers were there, apparently on their break. They were lounging around a table at the back, looking wilted and disheartened. After I ordered, I decided to give them a little encouragement, so I went to thank them for their singing.

Fanning themselves with menus, they perked up and accepted my praise gratefully.

Suddenly one of the men said, "Why don't you sing for *us*?"

I blinked. "You want *me* to sing for *you*?" I was sure I had misheard. These people were obviously professional musicians—why in the world would they want to hear *me* sing?

Another man nodded. "We've been singing for people all day," he said. "Nobody's sung for us."

I felt shy for a moment, and then decided to go ahead and do it. I don't have a great voice, but I've belonged to church choirs since I was a kid. I can sing. Besides, they did ask for it. And I wanted to hear one real carol that day, even if I had to sing it myself.

Discarding "Silent Night" as too obvious, I launched into "It Came upon the Midnight Clear."

Much to my satisfaction, I got all the notes right, even the tricky bit with "Peace on the earth, good will to men."

When I finished the first verse, I paused, and they sang the second verse to me. We finished the carol together. The other customers gave a round of applause.

My order was ready, so I returned to my table. Finishing their coffee, the carolers straggled out to the street and got back to work. Strains of "Jingle Bell Rock" and "Buh-Buh-Blue Christmas" drifted in whenever the door opened, but I wasn't interested. I was thinking only of our impromptu performance:

> *"When peace shall over all the earth*
> *Its ancient splendors fling,*
> *And the whole world give back the song*
> *Which now the angels sing."*

Merry Christmas, Angie. As long as peace is flinging its ancient splendors, let's hope it flings some on us.

Love,
Lynne

December 26, 1999

Dear Angie,

It's been another one of those Technicolor Christmases in Los Angeles, poinsettias and bougainvillea against the flat blue sky, bright as Mexico. The palm trees rattle their fronds in the eighty-degree breeze like tone-deaf sleigh bells. But I wasn't surprised when Mark announced his decision to buy an electric blanket at the after-Christmas sales.

Just the same, I didn't intend to let him get away with it. "Why on earth would you want one?" I asked.

"I can't get my bed warm at night."

Mark never can get warm. I don't use the heater as much in a whole year as he does in a month. He could easily raise orchids in his apartment, and I don't know why he doesn't. It would be a nice second income.

Living with Skeeter, I don't have any problem getting the bed warm. I suggested that Mark should get a cat instead of an electric blanket. Being a cat person is the only way to luxuriate in fur without getting Greenpeace on your case.

"Not big enough," he answered.

It's true—Mark is not a small man. One cat wouldn't do it.

"What about several cats?" I asked. "Like six?"

"I don't want six cats."

"What about one big one? Maybe a leopard?"

Mark has never owned a pet of any sort, and I don't think he's about to start now. The leopard, though, was far out, even for one of my ideas. For one thing, it's illegal to own wildlife in California. Also, there are practical considerations. The quantity of raw meat a leopard would need would probably strain an author's income. Then, too, the size of the litter box would be daunting. Not to mention that Mark would be hard-pressed to train such a creature. I don't picture him as a wild animal tamer, I really don't.

I was starting to think I needed help training Skeeter, but a book I got for Christmas has decided me otherwise. The book contains careful instructions for getting a cat off your favorite chair. These instructions involve the use of a broomstick, so your hands won't get shredded. What are they talking about, leopards? My technique with Skeeter is a lot simpler. I approach his chair, scoop him up, and tickle his tummy.

"Wanna share, Skeet?" I croon. "Wanna snuggle?"

I plop myself down in the chair with Skeeter on my lap. I pet him some more. He purrs. I haven't needed a broomstick yet. Maybe I should write a book.

If I became an author, would I need an electric blanket? Mark's going to the sales tomorrow. I think I'll tag along, just in case.

                    Love,
                    Lynne

December 30, 1999

Dear Angie,

    I'm not worried about Y2K and neither is Skeeter. Mark, too, has backed off about it, which is good. I was beginning to get tired of the subject.
    When I first heard about the problem a couple of years ago, I decided that, with all the money to be made in fixing it, everything would be fine. About a year ago, I did get a little nervous. I don't pretend to be a techie. People everywhere were talking so knowledgeably about what a terrible problem it was, so I started to think, *Well, what do I know?*
    But then an acquaintance with barely enough intelligence to find her mouth with her fork started sounding as technically sophisticated about it as everyone else. I decided it was baloney and lapsed into my usual apathy.
    Mark did enough worrying for both of us. He bought cases of bottled water—enough to float a small sailboat—and wanted me to go halves on a camping stove. I refused. In my backpacking days, I blew up two of those suckers. I'm convinced I'm haunted by The Curse of the Camping Stove. If the gas and electricity went off forever, I'd learn to make a fire by rubbing two sticks together.

Los Angeles is either the largest or the second largest city in the United States. I'm not going to match quarters about it at this point. But the idea that the utilities will go off strikes me as bizarre. If they did, though, the emergency services would manage something. There's even an informal emergency network. After one earthquake, two major breweries started bottling water and giving it away in areas where the mains were broken. A kid, hauling a couple of six packs home, was stopped by a policeman who hadn't heard anything about it. But some passersby soon cleared up the misunderstanding.

Skeeter is waiting for midnight, December 31, with some anticipation. He's indifferent to the coaches turning into pumpkins, but he really wants to see whether the footmen will turn into rats and mice. He's ready. And he has no trouble finding his mouth, although I haven't seen him use a fork. Yet.

Hope your New Year's is uneventful.

Love,
Lynne

January 5, 2000

Dear Angie,

    Melissa, my sister, took a basket of fancy foods to her son, Tony, as a New Year's present. The basket included smoked salmon, oysters wrapped in bacon, a cheese in red wax, an assortment of crackers and marmalade, and several kinds of chocolate truffles. She also included a large box of tissues for Tony's wife, who has a cold. "Gee, thanks, Mom," said Tony, accepting the basket. "Now we're ready for Armageddon."
    New Year's Eve passed without incident. Skeeter thought it was the end of the world, but that's because he doesn't like fireworks.
    To get his mind off it, I let him "help" take down the Christmas tree. As I removed the ornaments, he watched, fascinated. He pounced on the tree several times as I dragged it to the back door.
    Since he isn't allowed to go outdoors, I managed the next tasks without interference. Down in the yard, I cut off the tree limbs with pruning shears, sawed the trunk in two, and stuffed the whole mess into the green waste bin. When I returned to the living room, I

found Skeeter having a fine time playing in drifts of Christmas tree needles. I tried to sweep them up, but every time I collected them into a tidy pile, he jumped in and scattered them again.

I went to the laundry room for the dustpan. When I came back, Skeeter looked odd. I peered at him curiously and he guiltily spat out a mouthful of fir needles. It made me think of the first time I ate an artichoke. I hope I didn't look as ridiculous as Skeeter, but I probably did.

When I was growing up, our family budget didn't include fancy groceries. We ate simply. So when a college friend offered me an artichoke one evening at dinner, I had no idea what to do it.

I covertly watched as she pulled leaves off hers, dipped them in butter and nibbled at the ends. That seemed easy enough. I pulled, dipped, and nibbled too.

When I got to the choke, though, it was obvious a new procedure was needed. My friend had lost interest in her artichoke. I could see I would have to fake it.

So I ate the thing. It was hard going too, about as palatable as Christmas tree needles. My friend stared at me in astonishment as I gulped it down. I think it was obvious I wasn't used to fancy groceries.

Skeeter started batting the now-damp needles around the floor. I pulled out the vacuum, which got rid of him. That's *his* idea of Armageddon.

                        Love,
                        Lynne

January 10, 2000

Dear Angie,

    Decorating for Christmas is magical, but taking the decorations down is a dreadful chore. As I mentioned in my last letter, I dismantled the Christmas tree on New Year's Day. Skeeter, with unusual helpfulness, had already begun this task. I had been finding ornaments all week in surprise locations where he'd been playing with them. I can't blame Skeeter for thinking they're cat toys—they are similar.
    Not as similar as my original ornaments, though. When I got the Christmas tree for my first apartment, I had recently adopted my orange cat, Marmalade. In a flight of fancy, I decided to trim the tree with cat toys and stuffed mice.
    I searched for mice in all the pet and toy stores for miles around. I garnered a truly impressive collection, even an angel mouse for the treetop. Looking for garlands, I found what I thought was the perfect thing: a roll of iridescent white ribbon about three inches wide.
    I was completing this Yuletide masterpiece when my friend Patricia knocked at the door. I let her in and stepped back to admire my effect. Patricia was silent, and I slowly realized she was temporarily speechless. It

also dawned on me that my tree didn't look like I had imagined it would.

"It looks . . . infested," I said, after a few moments.

It did. Mice swarmed along all the branches and peeped from behind the lights. The tree was crawling with them.

"It certainly does," said Patricia. She seemed relieved she didn't have to produce admiration.

I looked again. "The garlands make it look like someone toilet-papered it," I added.

"They certainly do," agreed Patricia. She seemed stuck. I think we both were, at that point.

My tree this year was much less original. As I packed the ornaments for another year, rescuing a few from behind the sofa pillows, I noticed one of the garlands was missing. Skeeter is sure to have put it somewhere. It will turn up, probably when the minister comes to lunch, or Mark's mother—someone I want to impress. It could be worse, though. This one is obviously a Christmas-tree garland. It doesn't look a bit like toilet paper.

Love,
Lynne

January 15, 2000

Dear Angie,

Rain in southern California is unpredictable. Some winters it's so plentiful I think of Bill Cosby's Noah routine. On the other hand, years can go by with no rain, not one blessed drop. Water is rationed then. After you take a bath, you leave the water in the tub and ladle it out in buckets to flush the toilet.

This has been a dry year, but it rained this morning. Skeeter had never seen rain and didn't know what to think. He dashed from one closed window to another, balancing precariously on the windowsills. He made a new sound that probably meant "What in the world?"—a soft but high-pitched gargle.

He became unusually playful, too, leaping from one toy to another as if he hoped to extract the meaning of this new phenomenon from one of them. He also hid and pounced on my feet. I started the morning barefoot as usual, but soon donned slippers for my own protection.

It's funny, though, how some primitive sense tells you when you're about to be pounced on. I think I first noticed this one evening when I was about sixteen.

There was only one phone in my parents' New Orleans house—in their bedroom. When I started dating, I found this a problem. I told myself it was because my tête-à-têtes with my boyfriend were private, and they were. But my need to protect my privacy wasn't based on steaming passion, as I told myself. I suspected my parents would find my talk both poignant and hilarious—I didn't want my first efforts at lovers' conversation to be laughed at.

Instead, I used the phone in my father's garage woodshop for my nightly telephone trysts. I would talk by the hour if nobody stopped me. During one of these conversations, I intuited there was something behind me, about to pounce. The hair on the back of my neck stood up.

I turned around to find I was being stalked by a crawfish. It looked about the size of a lobster. Its claws were extended and snapping, fast closing in on my ankles.

I shrieked and chased the critter away with a broom. Then I went back to the phone and explained, but this wasn't easy. My boyfriend had been badly scared when I screamed. Now he was relieved, annoyed, and incredulous. Attacked by a crawfish? Did it have a gun?

Even that wasn't enough to make me use the house phone when I talked to my boyfriend, though I kept an eye out for marauding wildlife from then on. Being stalked is much less upsetting than being laughed at, when you're sixteen and in the throes of first love.

I've never heard of any other case of a crawfish attacking a human—till now I haven't been able to imagine what was on that one's mind. I'm starting to have a glimmering, though—the crawfish must have been the Skeeter of the arthropod world, set off by something beyond anyone's understanding. Rain, maybe.

Love,
Lynne

January 22, 2000

Dear Angie,

    Winter is not past, of course, even in Southern California, but "the rain is over and gone"—for now. For all the fretting, we got less than half an inch. The news media today are through with yesterday's fender benders and are back to talking about La Niña. I don't know why they can't use the frank, old-fashioned word "drought." It's always sufficed before.

    Skeeter's reaction to water falling out of the sky was a sharp increase in energy. I wish it affected me that way. He played furiously with his toys and even snitched one of mine, a hand carved wooden doll about six inches tall. When I came home from work, I found it on the floor where he'd been fooling with it. I played with dolls when I was little, but I've never heard of a cat doing it.

    As kids, my sister, Melissa, and I were doll-crazy. Our mother wouldn't let us have Barbies and glamour queens of that ilk. Instead we had Raggedy Anns, Toni dolls, stuffed animals, and a crowd of dollhouse inhabitants. Our Toni dolls had long lost their wigs by the time of my earliest memories. This, in our world, meant they were men. Having become enraptured with the King Arthur stories, we appointed the Toni dolls as

Lancelot and Galahad. My sister's plush dog did duty as a horse, as did an English Tigger of mine. The Toni dolls engaged in jousts on these unlikely mounts. I don't remember what they used as weapons.

The Raggedy Anns were Elaine and Guinevere. Since we were more interested in sword fighting than in either glamour or romance, my memories of the womenfolk are hazy.

Our grandmother had given us baby dolls, but these did not fit well into the Arthurian legend. The difficulty wasn't their appearance. A child who can pretend Raggedy Ann is Queen Guinevere would easily accept Betsy Wetsy as the Green Knight. The baby dolls had two insurmountable problems. The first was that we spoke lines for the characters. But just as we were about to intone something like, "Ye be of great chivalry and right hardy, why come ye not to cast me out of peril of death?"—the Green Knight would break in with *Ma-ma* and spoil the effect.

The other drawback was their trademarked attraction, namely their incontinence. We found their tendency to wet their tinfoil armor to be inauthentic and banished them to the toy box.

We built medieval towns in the backyard, using discarded cartons for castles and manors. Our pride and joy was a tall cylindrical container that had once held laundry detergent. This was the tower. In my subsequent architectural history studies, I was never to see photographs of chateaus without checking their pinnacles for the brand name *all*.

Sometimes we played Mad Hatter tea party with these same dolls, magically transformed into Lewis Carroll characters. Melissa once persuaded me to take a bite out of one of the china doll dishes in imitation of the story. Explaining that one to Mom was fun.

I took the doll away from Skeeter, but if he's following in my footsteps, he may soon chew the dishes. Next time it rains, I could find some tiny, tooth marked shards lying around. I'll be sure to wear shoes, just in case.

Love,
Lynne

January 26, 2000

Dear Angie,

    I visited the town of El Segundo today. I lived there when I first moved to southern California, but I hadn't been back for years. The place has changed, of course. It's getting built up now, and most of the old houses have been replaced by what people here call "McMansions." When I lived there, I had a tiny house, no more than five or six hundred square feet. There were dozens of those cottages in El Segundo then. They had big yards—mine stretched along half the block, behind the shallower lots on the cross street. At the back of my yard was a hedge, and this hedge had a gap, if you looked carefully.
    Through the gap was Mrs. Fairchild's yard. Her house was another of the small ones, actually a converted garage, and she lived alone in it. I'm not sure if I ever knew her first name. I wouldn't have used it if I had. I called her Mrs. Fairchild, as I knew she preferred.
    She had a married son, who visited her often and did as much for her as she'd allow. But she wanted to be independent. And she was.

I didn't feel responsible for her. But I thought a little neighborliness would be welcome. So I'd make my way through the hedge, sometimes with cookies, sometimes without. She probably baked better cookies than I did, but she accepted mine politely and chatted with me for a while. Mostly she talked about the town and about the past.

She had lived in the neighborhood for many years, not originally in the garage house but in another of the modest ones. I liked to listen to her memories. "Back in the twenties, we thought we'd soon be parking our own airplane in the driveway. Instead we got the Depression. We were so disappointed.

"My husband left when my son was a baby. Walked away one morning and never came back. I kept us going by cleaning houses, cleaned all the houses around here." She peered through her window. "The ones that used to be around here."

With her son grown and gone, most days she just talked to Buddy, her cat. He was a tabby tom, friendly enough if you scratched his favorite spots and knew better than to touch his tail. I never knew why he was sensitive about the tail. If it was touched, he performed a Jekyll-and-Hyde whirl from tabby to tiger and sank his teeth in the offending hand. He didn't do it to me, though. Mrs. Fairchild warned me in time.

She told me he'd first come up the drive, squalling and skinny, as a stray kitten. This was not easy to imagine. Buddy must have weighed twenty pounds when I met him. He'd gotten lost once when he was small, and she'd thought he was gone for good. But he came back and stayed. He and Mrs. Fairchild had stayed, and our two cottages had stayed, but now the town was changing around us. Changing fast.

I finally had to move away from El Segundo. My house was being torn down, as so many were, to make way for a much finer structure. I couldn't find anything else in town that I could afford. Today I tried to remember whether I said goodbye to Mrs. Fairchild before I left. I think so. I hope I did.

Her house is gone too now. I suppose she's gone as well. It would be tempting to think the neighborliness disappeared when the trophy houses were built. Tempting and a little cheap. The hedge is still there, and maybe the gap is too. You never could see it from the street.

Love,
Lynne

January 29, 2000

Dear Angie,

    Skeeter is not entirely happy about the way we live. For example, he doesn't like my going to work. With more justification, he disapproves of some of my attitudes. Most of my experience with animals is with dogs. In a relationship with a pet, I elect myself pack leader. Cats are not pack animals. Skeeter, a democrat, considers us equals and resents my bumptious ways.
    This is particularly true when it comes to food. I buy various kinds of food for Skeeter so he won't become too set on one type or flavor. I had a friend in high school whose cat, Sparkles, would eat nothing but Kitty Queen Tuna. No other brand would do, even people tuna. Kitty Queen Salmon would not do, either. My friend's family had Kitty Queen Tuna crises, when none could be found. "Did you try the all-night drugstore?" "We went there last time, remember? They don't have it." The cat probably would have starved before it ate anything else.
    My friend's mother had a strange relationship with the cat. She believed Sparkles to be the reincarnation of her own mother, long deceased. So the cat ruled the household. I am not going down that road with Skeeter.

A gauntlet has been thrown, though, regarding turkey. Till last week, he ate it with obvious enjoyment. The two cans I've given him this week have gone untouched. Someone said it might be spoiled, that I should smell it. A longtime vegetarian, I think meat always smells spoiled, but I gave it a whiff. Disgusting, but not rancid. I won't buy it again, though, if he feels that way.

This morning he got beef, which he accepted. In fact, he made a pig of himself. After breakfast he returned to the bedroom, belching alarmingly.

"Would Monsieur like a potato with the steak next time?" I asked. "Perhaps a small glass of red wine?" Monsieur looked interested. "A salad?" No sale.

I think I'll continue being pack leader. Like all despots, I perpetuate Skeeter's servitude by monopolizing the means to freedom: the checkbook, the car keys, the can opener.

It's unfair that I should be the leader just because I'm bigger and smarter and have opposable thumbs. But it's going to stay that way as long as I can manage it. If Skeeter is the reincarnation of my mother, she can learn to eat what she's given.

        Love,
        Lynne

February 5, 2000

Dear Angie,

Thanks for calling this morning. It was great to talk to you. Sorry about the ruckus in the background. It was Skeeter, of course. He resents it when I talk on the phone.

For a few minutes he waits, shifting from foot to foot like a kid. He has four feet to alternate among, though, so his performance is more interesting than any human's could possibly be. Eventually, he starts to chew the handset cord or, if I'm on the cordless, my arm. If that doesn't work, he runs around and caterwauls.

Sometimes he even puts his foot on the button and hangs the phone up. It looks deliberate to me. He may want me to get off the phone and pay attention to him, but it's also possible he wants to make a call.

I've had some experience with people wanting to use my phone, and I know how demanding they can be. When I was married, my husband, Allen, and I lived in a two-flat building in Baton Rouge. At least, it was supposed to be a two-flat. It had a third, bootleg unit tacked onto the back—probably a former service porch. Now it was a tiny bachelor apartment.

The girls in the bootleg apartment lived a bohemian life. They didn't bother me much, except having no telephone of their own, they often asked to borrow ours. This irritated me, not only because of the intrusion, but also because Allen all too obviously encouraged it—these girls were cute.

But even Allen was irritated one cold midnight when a knocking at the door roused us. He answered it and was confronted by an enraged older man.

"Where's my daughter?" the guy yelled.

Allen stared at him blankly. "Who?"

"Cynthia, my daughter! Where is she?" His voice boomed in the stillness of the sleeping neighborhood. He crowded the doorway, seemingly about to push his way in.

Allen was bewildered. Cynthia? Oh, one of the girls in the bachelor apartment. He sent the man back there, locked the door, and returned to bed. We laughed with relief and went back to sleep.

About an hour later, an even more insistent knocking woke us again. Allen went to the door. It wasn't the father this time—it was a shivering young man wearing nothing but a pair of cutoff jeans. He asked to come in and use the phone.

"What's going on?" said Allen. Since he wasn't talking to a cute girl, Allen had some inkling he was being imposed on.

"Cynthia's father came and beat on the door," said the boy. "I was there, so I pulled on my cutoffs and hid in the closet behind some clothes."

"So?" Allen still didn't see why the boy had knocked on our door.

"They got into a big argument. The old guy yelled: 'We're goin' back to Tennessee, Cynthia!' Then he jerked open the closet door and grabbed the clothes. There I was, hunkered on the floor."

"What did you say?" asked Allen.

"What was there to say? I jumped out and ran. I guess she's going back to Tennessee. I need to call someone to come get me."

We let him use the phone. As he'd put it, what was there to say?

I have lots to say to Skeeter about his antics when I'm on the phone, but I don't think he's listening.

Love,
Lynne

February 10, 2000

Dear Angie,

Not long ago, Mark said he thought my apartment looked uninhabited, more diorama than dwelling. He was referring to the combined effect of my neatness and my love of museum-quality wicker furniture. In his view, this produced an intimidating atmosphere, as if the interior decorator had only just left and might be coming back to check up.

My response was that his place looks unlived-in too. I countered his surprise by adding that most book warehouses *are* unlived-in. We both got a laugh from this, and it continues to be a joke, with variants such as, "Well, you have to admit, it looks lived-in today."

Now that Skeeter has become, in cat terms, a teenager, a decorator would probably be disappointed in me. The wicker is too valuable to give to Skeeter. But I'm not home during the day to prevent him from scratching it to ribbons. My solution has been to cover everything with blankets until he gets firmly fixed in the habit of using his scratching posts. Mark says my place, too, looks like a warehouse—the warehouse of a storage and transfer company. He's right, temporarily.

This is my solution to the furniture problem, but Skeeter is not a one-problem cat. Like teenagers of any species, Skeeter is busily testing my limits. He's obedient, for a cat—he comes when called, usually respects my "no," and is clean in his habits. Some typical teen problems were forestalled when I got him neutered. In certain ways, though, he's been a problem.

Some of my possessions especially incite Skeeter to mischief. One is an Amish quilt hanging above the bed. He likes to bat at it and explore the wall behind it. Heaven knows why—there's nothing there. Another is a phoenix kite on the wall by my desk. Its tail feathers are irresistible, also delicate. A third is a wind chime on a bracket within his reach. Skeeter plainly thinks it's an alarm clock. He bats it to get me up.

He does this with one eye on me—if he were human, he'd be sticking out his tongue. He knows his behavior annoys me.

I consulted a few friends who have cats. The advice I received was confusing. It ranged from letting him do whatever he wants, to swatting him hard.

I sifted the varied opinions and developed a workable program. When Skeeter is naughty, I tap him with one finger, gently but not caressingly. If he persists, he gets a time-out in the bathroom. This has in fact happened only a few times. Skeeter hates solitary, even for twenty minutes. He has adjusted his behavior to—barely—avoid this supreme penalty.

Of course, he tears up the bathroom while he's in there. I'm resigned to it—at least it makes it look slightly more lived-in.

                                        Love,
                                        Lynne

February 20, 2000

Dear Angie,

When I first met Mark, I thought I'd like to read one of the books he'd written. So I ordered a copy from one of the big bookstores. They were "out of stock," as they seem to be with everything I want.
Yesterday, I got a call from the store to tell me my book had come in. "What book?" I asked. It had been such a long time, I'd forgotten about it.
They gave me the title and author, and then I remembered.
Problem was, Mark gave me that book for Valentine's Day. Signed, of course, but also inscribed, "With all my love." Clearly, this was the copy I wanted.
Just as clearly, telling the exact truth to the bookstore clerk would have been a mistake. She would have thought I was a real nut case.
"It's been so long since I ordered the book, I got a copy from another source," I said, thinking fast.
She apologized and got off the phone, but it left me giggling all day. I giggled as I tidied the house and even in public, doing my errands. It goes to show, you just can't win. Now the bookstore clerk doesn't think I'm a nut case, but a lot of other people do.

One of the errands was the pet store. I got a collar and leash for Skeeter so I can take him for walks and terrorize the neighbors. He needs something to do besides wreck my apartment.

Love,
Lynne

February 29, 2000

Dear Angie,

We had our own sort of "leap" year celebration here today, brought on by my putting a harness and leash on Skeeter. The cat book said to put the harness on first, to give him a chance to get used to it. After about an hour, he realized he couldn't get it off, so he withdrew under the bed to pout. I offered treats, but he snubbed me.

When he finally came out, I clipped on the leash. The book said to let him get used to it by dragging it around. I don't think Skeeter had read the book.

He tore around the apartment, back and forth. His paws drummed on the wood floors. The downstairs neighbor pounded on the ceiling, making things worse. Another neighbor's dog started barking, probably convinced a cat invasion was at hand. Some Million Cat March, maybe. There was far too much noise for just one.

Skeeter revved up a whole other notch. He was moving too fast to catch now, so I couldn't do anything about taking off the harness and leash. I could only watch.

He leaped onto the sideboard, scattering plates and cups like bowling pins. It's a good thing I'd bought unbreakable dishes in case of earthquakes. I'd give Skeeter's performance an eight on the Richter scale.

Mark knocked at the back door, wanting to know what the ruckus was about. I let him in and we cornered Skeeter and took the offending articles off him.

Poor man, he probably thought he was going to get some writing done when he moved in here.

Love,
Lynne

March 10, 2000

Dear Angie,

I can't understand why Skeeter is so interested in flies. He'll do anything to get one. Anything. He chases them from room to room with as much enthusiasm as if they were flying beefsteaks. He makes a strange noise during this pursuit, a kind of clicking sound.

There seems no point to it. Even if he catches one, the calories gained by swallowing it can't equal those expended in pursuit. Mark says the function of the exercise is to refine Skeeter's hunting skills, and he's probably right. Skeeter's hunting skills could use some refinement.

Yesterday Skeeter flung himself onto the back of the couch, trembled on the edge for a moment, eyes on an elusive insect, then fell back, tush over teakettle, landing on the floor with a thump. He looked around to see if anyone had noticed. I tried to look unaware but couldn't help laughing. He stalked away, mortally insulted.

I shouldn't have laughed, though. No fair. No one laughed the day I skated down the cliff on my butt.

San Pedro is a seacoast town. At the edge of the Pacific is a cliff, perhaps seventy-five feet high. I was wandering on the cobble beach below the cliff one day when I saw something interesting: an elongated flexible cone or seedpod that was new to me. Looking up, I saw that more of these littered the slope, dropping from a tree at the cliff's edge. My sister was taking a basketry course and was interested in such materials. I decided to send her some of the cones.

Climbing the cliff was easy, even gathering cones as I went. But when I turned around, I realized something. It's harder to go down.

I was looking at a nearly sheer cliff, stones at the bottom, and ocean breakers very close. Along the cliff top, a chain-link fence extended as far as I could see. No escape there.

I abandoned my pride and skated down on my rear, blistering it in the fast descent and rubbing a noticeably-positioned hole in my clothing. At the bottom, I looked around to see if anyone had noticed. If any fool had been down there laughing, I would have throttled him. As it was, I stalked away in the shreds of my dignity and the shreds of my jeans.

So I should have been more sympathetic when Skeeter wiped out on the couch. It's always funnier when it happens to someone else.

>   Love,
>   Lynne

March 20, 2000

Dear Angie,

If I'd known I'd be living with Skeeter, I wouldn't have bought an alarm clock. I no longer use one. He yowls me awake each morning at dawn, whether I need it or not.

But before I met Skeeter, I thought I'd need a clock. I tried several. An ordinary alarm blasted me out of sleep too harshly, so I bought a clock radio. I was pleased with it till the day my waking time coincided with the news. "THE WORLD IS NOW CLOSER TO NUCLEAR WAR THAN AT ANY TIME IN THE PAST THIRTY YEARS!" This was not what I had in mind.

Other clocks came and went. Some ticked too loudly for me to sleep, which solved the wake-up problem in a way. I struggled along until I found the clock in the New Age store.

It's a satin-black wood triangle, oddly appropriate on top of my bookcase with an Amish quilt on the wall behind it. The quilt too has black triangles in it.

It wakes me with a simple soft chime, insistently repeated if I don't turn off the alarm. I could have gotten a version that repeats affirmations in my voice, but decided the chime was enough. Some days, you don't want any damn affirmations.

The clock is getting dusty now that Skeeter shares my mornings. His 5:30 cries are sure as sunrise, though at this season, prior to it. Like the clock, he repeats at ever-shorter intervals till I get up. How does he know what the time is, I wonder? He may have an alarm watch, like many people who attend the same events that I do. Their alarms for this and that inevitably sound at the most dramatic moment of each performance, the most solemn part of every funeral.

Or perhaps he's subscribed to some wake-up call service, for which I'll eventually receive a bill. Knowing Skeeter, that seems likely.

Love,
Lynne

March 31, 2000

Dear Angie,

Skeeter begs for my oatmeal every morning, but he wouldn't eat any if I gave it to him. He asks for lots of things he doesn't want. He stands at his overflowing food bowl and caterwauls, just to test the service around here. He nags me to let him go out on the balcony and usually lasts about three minutes before demanding, equally loudly, to be let back in.

Asking for what you don't really want isn't the greatest idea. Things can work out oddly, as they did for George.

George was a guy who lived near me when I was in college. I didn't know him well. One summer morning I was about to go to the swimming pool when a friend called. She asked me to deliver a message to George, who didn't have a phone. Since it was on my way, I agreed to do it.

That was the summer I wore white everything. Someone had told me it was "my" color, and I probably did look good in it, with my pale skin and dark hair. At nineteen, you don't wear "your" color once in a while—you make it into a fetish. My getup must have looked like a nurse's uniform, but I thought I was glamorous—the woman in white.

I had white dresses, white shorts, white blouses, and white everything else. I must have used more Clorox that summer than in my entire life since. My apartment reeked of it. I bleached everything to the point of destruction, wanting the whites as stunning as possible. And they were.

So when I headed to the pool that morning, I was wearing a white cover-up dress over a white bikini. I knocked on George's door, and he hollered for me to come in.

George's place was one room, and he was still in bed. "Oh, hi," he said. "Make yourself comfortable. Take your clothes off."

With a bikini under my dress, I decided to do it. It hadn't occurred to me how like underwear the white bikini looked.

"Sure," I said, and took off the cover-up.

By then, George was hiding under the blanket, trapped in his own apartment and in his own joke. I told him it was a bikini, delivered the message, and left. I hope I didn't leave him with any lasting traumas, but I never knew. He avoided me after that, for some reason. Maybe he didn't like white.

So Skeeter had better watch out. When you ask for something you don't want, you sometimes get it.

Love,
Lynne

April 8, 2000

Dear Angie,

I started a cold last week, but it went away without doing much. It's just as well. Skeeter has neither the gluteal muscles to stand upright, nor the opposable thumbs to carry trays with healing foods like Chinese hot-sour soup or lemony tea. The truth is, if Skeeter did have the necessaries, he still wouldn't carry trays. He'd be out the door in a flash, borrowing the car.

Lord knows what it would do to my car insurance rates to add an adolescent male to my policy. Would it make any difference that he's neutered?

The City of Los Angeles seems to think it would. The city council is considering a proposal to tax unneutered animals. I suppose they'd ask for a certificate from the vet, but my heated imagination pictures something else. I see an army of pet inspectors, lifting cat tails to make sure there's not more there than there's supposed to be. Take your dachshund for a walk, a man from the city will show a badge and make you take off the dog's little plaid coat, so he can get a better look.

I had similar thoughts a few years ago when the council passed the ordinance about "picking up after your pet," as they so delicately phrased it. I imagined they'd have to hire short undercover agents to hide behind fire hydrants. "Freeze! This is a bust!" The dog's hind leg would already be raised, though, so he couldn't put his paws behind his head. The owner would have to take care of that part.

I can't blame the city for trying to do something about the problems uncontrolled animals can cause. On the other hand, the cleanup ordinance didn't work well, and I doubt this one will either. It will be another bureaucratic idiocy, costing much and accomplishing next to nothing. Angelenos have gotten used to those over the years. They're as persistent as colds, and the remedies aren't much more effective than hot lemony tea.

Love,
Lynne

April 22, 2000

Dear Angie,

For all his feistiness, Skeeter is wary of company. It's my fault.

When I first moved here, the landlady said I could have a cat. She knew of a stray in her nephew's neighborhood and drove me over to the empty house where this cat was said to hang out, so I could see it. I knew what I was looking for: a calm adult female.

I didn't see any cat. "Kitty-kitty," I called, tentatively. A tabby-and-white kitten appeared from under a bush, ran down the driveway, and threw itself into my arms. It was less than half-grown. Although I'm not an expert at sexing cats, a look at the relevant areas suggested it was a male.

It licked my face. The deal was done.

So Skeeter was not afraid of strangers when he came to me. As I said, it's my fault.

To begin with, I don't have many visitors. I live at the extreme southern tip of Los Angeles, so my friends tend to meet me places, rather than drive to the end of the freeway and beyond. Also, I'm studying for professional exams, not socializing as much as usual.

Skeeter's early experiences with strangers were not the best, either. A conscientious owner, I immediately took him to the vet's, first for kitten shots, then for neutering. This involved a series of excursions when he was imprisoned in a cat carrier and taken to see strangers, all of whom did uncomfortable things to him.

The final straw came when, for a minor indisposition of Skeeter's, I decided to spare him the trip in the carrier. I arranged with a vet who makes house calls. She came to the apartment, examined Skeeter, and decided there wasn't much wrong with him. Told me to give him bland food for a few days, which turned out to be good advice.

But Skeeter's suspicions had been confirmed. He now regards every visitor as someone who may be carrying a rectal thermometer. I guess I'd hide under the bed myself if I expected guests to behave like that.

When people come to visit, they always want to meet him—I don't know why. You'd think they'd be warned off by the stories I tell. They make a special trip beyond the end of the freeway, knock on my door, and expect to meet the cat. I give them coffee and cookies and introduce them to Mark. But if Skeeter doesn't put in an appearance, they seem disappointed. Some people don't know when they're lucky.

I've even been accused of inventing him. But if I could make up a character as good as Skeeter, I'd call Mark's agent in a minute. I'd write a series of best sellers and forget about the professional exams. I'd have company all day long. Skeeter could damned well get used to it.

Speaking of company, when are *you* coming to visit?

Love,
Lynne

April 29, 2000

Dear Angie,

I've seen a couple of movies that featured "outtakes" as part of the comedy. I tried taking some pictures of Skeeter last week, and now I'm wondering whether the outtakes from this effort might also be worth keeping.

I borrowed the office camera, since I wanted to post the pictures on the Internet and don't have a digital camera of my own. I don't know much about cameras or photography, but I learned a bit. The office camera, chosen for architectural photography, is much less satisfactory for taking pictures of a cat. Particularly Skeeter.

The problem is that after you push the button to take the picture, there is a pause of about a second before the thing actually works. This is fine for buildings. If they move noticeably within a second, you have more serious problems than a poor photograph. Skeeter, on the other hand, never stays still for more than the blink of an eye.

He was cooperative about posing, in his way. He made funny faces for me as I pushed the button. But the photo showed only the back of his head as he turned away, satisfied his performance had been recorded.

I dangled a catnip mouse, and he obligingly did a somersault. That time, I got a good shot of his nether parts as he completed the maneuver.

Another time, he held a pose, but I was rewarded only with the triple beep that means the disk is full.

Further attempts to immortalize Skeeter resulted in enough outtakes to fill my second disk. The most interesting was the shot in which he had left the frame before the camera got around to recording him. It was a fetching portrait of my bedspread, though, suitable for framing.

Twice, he pounced on the camera right after I pressed the button, apparently taking the dangling strap for the tail of a large rodent. These shots, too, provided interesting outtakes.

I finally caught on to the problem: given anything much to do, Skeeter is a lot faster than my camera *or* me. I removed the fun stuff, all his toys, and also my afghan, which he was chewing with ominous delight. I rolled the camera strap and hid it in one hand. In the brief interval in which he considered his options for wreaking havoc in the absence of anything to wreak it on, I got one useful photo, the one I eventually posted.

I'm going back to architectural photography. I was told on one occasion the building I was restoring was a cathouse, but it didn't pounce on my camera even once. Meantime, I have some remarkable outtakes of Skeeter. I'm not sure what I'll do with them yet, but I think I should save them, just in case.

    About your visit: Could you make it early to mid-June?

Love,
Lynne

May 2, 2000

Dear Angie,

I've shuffled the furniture around to make the living room more comfortable for a houseguest. Also, it looks better this way. I don't rearrange nearly as much as I used to. That's a good thing, because it makes Skeeter uneasy.

He walked around afterwards sniffing everything. Then he looked me in the eye and performed a few claw-sharpening maneuvers. I've read that these are a means of marking territory. I suppose he has to reassert his ownership of anything that has moved. Otherwise, it might be mistaken for mine.

I was uneasy myself on a furniture-moving occasion years ago when my friend Mandy redecorated for me. I suppose Mandy was doing me a favor, since she's a professional decorator. It wasn't her fault it didn't work out.

At the time, I lived in a tiny house that I had arranged to my liking. Mandy visited one day and decided the living room could be better. And I thought, well, what do I know? *I'm* no decorator.

She started modestly. "I think the room would look better if you switched this table with that one," she suggested. It wasn't much work, so I tried it. The effect was OK. Maybe even an improvement. I wasn't sure.

She didn't leave me much time to mull it over. Right away, she suggested I move the bookcase to the other side of the room. This called for removing the books. I may have gotten sidetracked looking at a couple of them. When I looked up, moving day had come. Furniture, lamps, and assorted objects were in a tumble in the middle of the room.

"I need some help with this stuff," Mandy panted. "It's heavy."

It was. I was in the middle of my Mission Oak period. I didn't have much furniture in that little place, but what I had weighed a ton. I got up and helped. I lifted, strained, and heaved. When things attained a semblance of order, Mandy studied the effect.

"I think the clock would look better on the bookcase," she said, whisking it to the new location. You don't do that with a pendulum clock. It throws the balance off. But it was too late to say so.

She didn't like the new arrangement either, so she adjusted it, piece by piece. Finally, she was satisfied. "There!" she said. "This is so much more *you*."

The furniture was back exactly where I'd had it. No lasting harm was done, except to the clock, which had to be professionally repaired. I stopped being stiff and sore within a few days.

Next time someone offers to redecorate me, I'm going to give them a long look, the one I've learned from Skeeter. Then I'm going to sharpen my fingernails on each piece of furniture, to assert my ownership. If that doesn't establish my territory, I don't know what will.

June 20 would be great for your visit. Let me know about your reservations, and I'll meet you at the airport. Public transit is not going to work from LAX to San Pedro. As they say, you can't get there from here, not on the bus.

I'll set up vacation time at work. How long can you stay?

Love,
Lynne

May 12, 2000

Dear Angie,

    I put Skeeter on his leash this morning for our first adventure into the unsuspecting world. We sat on the front porch and surveyed the neighborhood. Representatives of the neighborhood surveyed us back—several cats, a few joggers, and some kids on bikes.
    This area of San Pedro is called Whiskey Flats, for no reason I can understand. It's hilly and there's no whiskey in sight. The rule in San Pedro used to be "Don't go east of Gaffey," but I think that must have changed. Here we are, one block east of Gaffey, and it's a nice neighborhood.
    It was much tougher when I first lived in this area ten years ago. A few of my friends were horrified when I moved to San Pedro. But I have a fair amount of experience in transitional neighborhoods. I like them. In my opinion, it's the rich areas that are truly dangerous. Why would muggers hang around here? A sensible thief would go to Brentwood, not waste time in Whiskey Flats.
    I lived in a similar area when I was in graduate school. This was in San Francisco, and I'm sure the neighborhood is far beyond my means now. But when I

lived there, it was marginal. Not slummy, I wouldn't say that, but it could have gone either way.

I rented a room from Katy, who owned a two-story brown shingle house, built in 1906 after the earthquake. It had bay windows, fireplaces, and stained glass. Most other houses on the block were about the same vintage, not as well kept, but not bad. A vacant lot next door was choked with wild fennel and sage. Directly above us at the crest of the hill were a few foundations where buildings had been torn down. Since the view from there was spectacular, new buildings were due soon. Our street was dead-end, paved with its original granite blocks. It was too steep for conventional paving. The sidewalk was a concrete staircase.

Katy was justifiably proud of her house. She was unsurprised and happy to agree when she was approached with a request for its use on the TV show "The Streets of San Francisco."

The filming went without a hitch. Katy was ecstatic. The night of the house's television debut, she alerted friends all over the country.

And it appeared, but not in the way she had imagined. It was presented as part of the ghetto from which the heroine was struggling to escape. In one memorable scene on our front porch, she gestured toward the house.

"I want to get out of this place," she said. "I want to make something of my life. I want to be a teacher."

Whiskey Flats is on about the same level as Katy's section of San Francisco, but several teachers live here, as well as a few computer types, entrepreneurs, salespeople, and one architectural consultant—me. And Skeeter, little demon that he is. I hope the joggers didn't take one look at him and say, "There goes the neighborhood." But I couldn't blame them if they did.

Love,
Lynne

May 20, 2000

Dear Angie,

For once, Skeeter accepted his harness and leash this morning. I'm always relieved when he doesn't resist, since my record of getting restraints on animals is mixed. My brother, Jim, can witness to that.

When I was in high school and Jim was about nine, he had a dachshund named Happy. One day I decided to take the dog for a walk and got her collar and leash from Jim's room. Happy was willing, even eager. But I couldn't figure out how to use the collar.

It was an ordinary dog collar, a straight piece of chain with a ring at each end. I tried hooking the leash to both rings, but it made far too big a loop, and I was sure Happy could get it off. In a flash of brilliance, I solved the problem. One loop must go through the other. I tried this and was confused when it didn't work. It had to be the answer, but the loops were the same size. Thinking again, I got the pliers, flattened one ring, and passed it through the other so the collar made a noose. I applied the pliers once more, making the flattened ring more or less round. Then I attached the leash and took Happy for her walk.

Later, when Jim came home, a wail emerged from his room: "Who ruined my dog collar?"

I explained what I'd done. He looked at me like I was crazy, then demonstrated the trick of passing the chain through the loop to make the noose. It wouldn't have occurred to me to do that if I'd worked on it for months.

I was born with my fair share of gifts, but mechanical ability is not one of them. I think I can claim to be free of it. Jim and I are grown now, but he occasionally reminds me I owe him a dog collar.

Considering my limitations, it's a good thing Skeeter doesn't create any extra challenges when I put on his hardware. The treat he gets for cooperating with me probably has a lot to do with it. Sometimes I wonder whether the animal at the end of my leash is a cat or a pig.

An article I read recently claims that using food rewards is wrong. The authors, a couple of professional animal trainers, say it's better if animals perform for praise only. They think praise reinforces the trainer's authority, while a treat is simply a bribe.

It's a bribe all right, but they have not met Skeeter, who is definitely on the take. Training Skeeter isn't a question of what I'll stoop to. It's a question of what works, and treats do, at least for now.

On the other hand, I wouldn't be surprised if Skeet reveals before long that goodies are not enough.

He'll probably soon be asking for small but regular deposits to a Bahamian bank account. And he'll get them—the same day Jim gets a new dog collar.

>Love,
>Lynne

June 5, 2000

Dear Angie,

It's good you can stay through July 4, because there's a block party in the afternoon. I'm not sure what's on the agenda, but it should be fun. There's a fireworks show at the beach in the evening too.

If I can leash-train Skeeter well enough by that time, we can take him to the party, but not to the fireworks, of course. I've been struggling with the leash almost every day. Some days I think he's catching on, and some days I don't.

Mark came downstairs and watched us awhile this morning. Skeeter has passed the point where he sits on my lap and trembles. Now he caroms around like a yo-yo. I'm not sure that counts as progress. Yo-yo was never one of my favorite games.

Mark, you may remember, has never had a pet. He hadn't thought about them much, either. He had always seen dogs trot along nicely on the leash and couldn't understand why Skeeter won't.

The subject of dogs and cats is a large one, but I tried to sum it up. "Dogs are more or less rational. They're emotionally so similar to people that they're used in psychological experiments. Cats are all emotion, no control. Dealing with a dog, to put it crudely, is like dealing with a person who's a bit dumb. Dealing with a cat is like dealing with a person who's more than a bit crazy."

There's also a saying, "Never try to out-stubborn a cat," but that's exactly what you have to do, of course. In training any animal, the real question is, who's going to give up first?

It won't be me. I am blessed—or cursed—with a stubbornness verging on perversity. You may have noticed I have pierced ears but never wear fancy earrings. The truth is, I didn't want pierced ears, but a boyfriend in high school told me, "Don't you ever dare pierce your ears"—so I had to. At least, at sixteen I thought I had to. I'm glad he didn't tell me not to tattoo "Mother" on my shoulder, with decorations of American flags and eagles. It wouldn't have looked good with my summer clothes.

Speaking of clothes, bring a few long-sleeved things and a sweater. California is less summery than Chicago, even when the temperature is higher. It feels cooler because of the dryness and the sea breeze. Also, nights are chilly just about all year.

I'm getting excited about your visit. I can hardly wait.

                        Love,
                        Lynne

June 12, 2000

Dear Angie,

    I guess this will be my last letter before your trip, but I'll call the day before to make sure we have our plans straight. Melissa, my sister, says she can take you to O'Hare. She'll call you to work out the details.
    I'll meet you at the gate at LAX. That place is a loud, confusing maze. I wouldn't be surprised if some visitors wander around the airport for their whole holiday, whimpering pitifully. Maybe there are special St. Bernards, looking for the lost and overwhelmed, bearing casks of Margaritas around their necks.
    Although, come to think of it, California-style Margaritas might make things worse. I encountered Margaritas for the first time when I moved here before to go to college. While I was unpacking, hot and thirsty, someone came over with a pitcher of what I thought was limeade. I chugged a couple of tall glasses before I realized it wasn't.
    That was the most unusual move of my life. I didn't remember the next morning where I had put anything, and it took about six months to find it all. The airport St. Bernards had better stick with brandy.

You won't need them, though. I'll be right at the gate.

                        Love,
                        Lynne

2
Dear Melissa

June 21, 2000

Dear Melissa,

Angie arrived in one piece yesterday. Thanks for taking her to the airport. She had a good flight, but we did get messed up at LAX. The airline posted the wrong arrival gate, but what did I know? I waited there patiently. Nobody showed up, even when the monitor said the flight had arrived. I finally grabbed the attention of an airline employee, who told me the gate had been switched. Uh-oh.

Luckily, Angie and I both carry cell phones, so I called her. I felt dorky, walking though the airport while giving my location. "OK, now I'm at the south end, that's the left end, of gate 88." Out of embarrassment, I was looking down. In fact, I wasn't looking where I was going. I plowed right into Angie, who was doing the same thing with her phone. We hung up, then hugged.

When we got home, Skeeter did his usual trick of hiding under the bed. Angie psyched him out in a minute. She pretended to be completely uninterested in him. He's used to people almost standing on their heads, coaxing him to come out. Angie just sat in the living room and talked to me. Skeeter was in her lap within fifteen minutes. She condescended to pet him and gave him a cat treat she had brought for the occasion. She has his number.

I don't know what will happen when she leaves. He'll probably pack a tiny suitcase and expect me to buy him a ticket to Chicago. I'm not sure Chicago is ready, either. The Windy City survived Al Capone and even Mayor Daley, but I doubt it's ready for Skeeter.

Love,
Lynne

June 30, 2000

Dear Melissa,

Angie surprised me. Everyone wants to see the ocean as soon as they get here, and she did want to see it. But first she wanted to visit the place I found Skeeter. I wasn't sure anymore exactly where it was.

"Why do you want to see that?" I asked. "It's an ordinary house."

"Just in case," she answered. I didn't know what she meant. Maybe she thought another Skeeter-cat might jump out of that bush. I've heard that lightning does sometimes strike twice in the same place. But what would she do if one did? She can't possibly want a cat like Skeeter.

Because he's been awful—that goes without saying—but not in the way I prepared her for.

The fact is, Skeeter has developed a crush on Angie. It would be funny, if he weren't so hard to put up with. He hides and waits, then pounces on her feet. He scrambles onto her lap at dinner and tries to grab her food. The way he does this is curious. He seems to think she can't see him because he's under the table. However, apart from noticing a paw hooking onto her plate, Angie could hardly miss him. The tabletop is glass.

Skeeter's disgrace extends beyond dinner hour. He spends nights in the kitchen now. I never have been able to sleep in the same room with Skeeter, and he's twice as bad with Angie. After the first night of having her ears chewed and her feet pounced on, she came to breakfast with circles under her eyes and a request that Skeeter bunk somewhere else.

We did get to the beach yesterday—in fact, to all the beaches. We have a sand beach for swimming, a cobble one for gazing out to sea, a salt marsh, and a sailboat marina. And a real fishing harbor, not a tourist attraction. Fishing boats have set out from it for a century or more, crewed mostly by the same families, generation after generation.

She was as indignant as I am about the feral cats. People dump them at the ocean. I guess they rationalize that the cats will fish. Since deep-sea fishing requires large boats with expensive gear, the likelihood that a cat could do it is slight. And the fishermen don't dump fish parts around the harbor for cats to scavenge. It's not allowed.

A local group of cat lovers catches harbor cats, has them neutered, and then releases them. They feed them twice a day and go to great trouble to take care of them. But they say, as soon as they get the population under control, more cats are dumped, and they have to start over.

That's the sad side of the beach, but we mostly had fun. Angie bought Skeeter some fish at a local market to make up for not staying home.

He'll probably be expecting a small offering now every night when I get home from work. And he'll want me to poach the damn thing in Chablis, too, while my own frozen dinner spins in the microwave. I'd better put my foot down. Enough is enough.

Love,
Lynne

July 5, 2000

Dear Melissa,

    I put Angie on the plane this morning. Her sister-in-law is picking her up at O'Hare, so I didn't have to ask you to do it.
    Yesterday was crazy. I am in shock. The block party started early and loud. We went to investigate and discovered there would be a potluck lunch in the closed-off street. So we went back inside to make cookies and sandwiches.
    Mark made a pasta dish, his specialty. I don't know what's in it, and I'm not sure I want to know. It's good.
    Just before noon, we took our goodies down to the tables in the street. I had no idea so many people lived on this block. There were kids weaving in and out on skateboards, adults comparing recipes, teenagers looking above-it-all. The food was great. San Pedro is a multiethnic community, and we had delicacies from all over the world.
    During lunch, we left Skeeter inside. But afterwards there were events, from three-legged races to a raffle. And there was—are you ready for this?—a neighborhood pet show.

We went upstairs and got Skeeter, and for once he behaved OK on his leash. Cats were first, then dogs, then other pets. The dogs were lining up as the cat parade was starting, and Skeeter swiped one of them right on the nose. I apologized to the owner, but I was proud of Skeeter. It was a dog that barks constantly. I wish I could have swatted him myself.

Skeeter eyed the other cats warily. I'm not sure he knows he *is* a cat, though I'm certain he doesn't think he's a human. He may think he's a one-of-a-kind creature, and if he does, he's right.

We paraded along the block for the neighbors' benefit. Skeeter had to be dragged at first, getting a laugh, but he cooperated after a few steps. Nearing the end of the block, I thought we were home free. Then we saw the boy sitting next to a cardboard box.

He had a hand-lettered sign, "Kittens Free to Good Homes." Well, I knew I didn't want one of those. Skeeter was more than enough.

Unfortunately, Skeeter had other ideas. I have heard stories about neutered male cats getting motherly, but I'd never seen it. Skeeter adopted one of those kittens himself, a little calico with a pink nose. He licked it, purring, and wouldn't leave.

I knew the landlady wouldn't let me have another cat. She was stretching a point for Skeeter. But Mark, at my elbow, was likewise smitten with the calico kitty. That little girl cat must've had something. I wish I knew what.

"Well, the landlady can hardly tell me I can't have a cat when she let you and Armando have one," said Mark, scooping up the kitten. Skeeter kept a nervous eye on Mark. He wanted it clearly understood that this kitten was his.

I looked over at Angie, but she didn't look back. She was absorbed in another kitten, an orange tabby male. I could not believe my eyes. She was taking the kitten and thanking the boy.

"Angie," I said, wondering if magic mushrooms or something had been in the sandwiches, "You can't take that cat back to Chicago."

"Well," she said, "I've decided to move here. I like it better than Chicago, and you know very well that place we worked is awful. I can do a lot better here, and I like the climate better. I'm tired of spending half the year up to my butt in snow."

"Isn't this kind of sudden?" I asked.

"Just like you did it," she answered, snuggling the kitten. "Can I stay with you awhile when I get back with my stuff?"

"Yes," I said, "but what are you going to do with the cat?"

"Well," she said—(I'm beginning to be gun-shy about that word)—"you'll keep it until I get back, won't you?"

I was cornered. I wanted Angie to move here, but another cat? "Yes," I said.

In a way, it's not so bad. Skeeter doesn't like the orange cat, but Skeeter is staying with Mark now—or rather, with Mark and that little calico heartbreaker. So I only have Angie's kitten.

He's a real devil. I wouldn't have thought anyone could make Skeeter look well behaved, but Angie's kitten manages it.

This arrangement won't be for long, though. Angie will be in California in a few weeks. When she gets here, Mark and I are going to combine our two apartments and live together. Maybe we'll move to a house eventually—if we can rent one where we can have two cats.

Love,
Lynne

About the Author

Formerly from San Pedro, California, Anne L. Watson now lives in Olympia, Washington, with her husband and fellow author, Aaron Shepard, and her one cat, Skeeter, who manages to be more than enough. Please visit them at **www.annelwatson.com**.

CPSIA information can be obtained at www.ICGtesting.com
Printed in the USA
LVOW08s2041200816

501188LV00001B/82/P

9 780938 497516